KU-024-985

He's the Prince of Pranks!

PRINCE JAKE

Swordfights and Slimeballs!

SUE MONGREDIEN ✹ MARK BEECH

ORCHARD BOOKS

He's the Prince of Pranks!

PRINCE JAKE

Swordfights and Slimeballs!

FOR MARTIN – THANKS FOR ALL
YOUR BRILLIANT IDEAS!
S.M.

FOR MRS SOUTHERN,
MY FIRST EVER ART TEACHER
AND MY INSPIRATION
M.B.

CAVAN COUNTY LIBRARY
ACC No. C/255597
CLASS NO. 35-8
INVOICE NO. 8923 IES
PRICE €8.11

ORCHARD BOOKS
338 Euston Road, London NW1 3BH
Orchard Books Australia
Level 17/205 Kent St, Sydney, NSW 2000

First published in 2008 by Orchard Books
First paperback publication in 2009
Text © Sue Mongredien 2008
Illustrations © Mark Beech 2008

The rights of Sue Mongredien to be identified as the author
and Mark Beech to be identified as the illustrator of this work
have been asserted by them in accordance with
the Copyright, Designs and Patents Act, 1988.
A CIP catalogue record for this book is available from the British Library.

ISBN HB 978 1 40830 279 8
ISBN PB 978 1 84616 616 7

HB 1 3 5 7 9 10 8 6 4 2
PB 1 3 5 7 9 10 8 6 4 2

Printed in Great Britain by
CPI Antony Rowe, Chippenham, Wiltshire

Orchard Books is a division of Hachette Children's Books
an Hachette Livre UK company.
www.hachettelivre.co.uk

CHAPTER ONE

CAVAN COUNTY LIBRARY

Prince Jake clasped the hilt of the silver sword, his eyes locked on the enemy before him. "You've done it now," he hissed, taking a step forward. "You should never have come here." He raised the sword and pointed it menacingly. "Now it's time to *pay*!"

"Wait!" came the scream. "Please – I beg you! Show some mercy!"

"No chance, loser," snarled Jake. He

swung the sword through the air, the heavy silver blade swishing, and...

"Prince Jake! Prince *Jake*! Are you listening?"

Jake jerked out of his daydream just as his sword sliced through an enemy neck and blood splattered everywhere.

Rats.

He wasn't fighting off the enemy after all. He didn't even have a whopping great silver sword in his hand. He was still here in the royal school room, with his governess Ms Prudence droning on.

Double rats!

Ms Prudence – or the Prune, as Jake always called her – stood there with a grim expression on her face, her mouth in a steely line. "Well?" she snapped.

Time for some major fibbing, thought Jake. "Um...yes," he said. "I *was* listening. I was just...um...thinking about what you said," he went on, vaguely. He racked his brain for the last thing he'd heard her say. "About bowing, and that," he tried.

"*Bowing?* We were talking about greetings twenty minutes ago!" the Prune told him, glaring through her half-moon spectacles. "Kindly pay attention for the rest of the lesson, Your Highness!"

Jake rolled his eyes at his younger brother, Prince Ned, as the Prune started chalking something up on the board. ROYAL MANNERS, he read.

Ugh. Manners. Bor-ing! How was he supposed to even *think* about manners when in just five minutes' time he was going to have his very first swordfighting lesson?

Jake grinned at the thought. Swordfighting – how cool was that? It was so brilliant that his mum, the Queen, had arranged for the Olympic swordfighting champion to come to the Moranian castle to give Jake, Ned and their older sister, Princess Petunia, lessons. Jake could hardly *wait* to get his hands on a real sword and start swishing it around!

"Now," said the Prune, fixing Jake with an icy glare. "Banqueting table manners. Let's start with cutlery…"

No, let's start with cutting off your head, Prune-features, Jake thought with a groan, stealing a look at the clock. Just four minutes to go…

♔ ♔ ♔

After what seemed more like four *hours,* the Prune glanced at her watch, and told them that the lesson was over. "Yesss! Time for swordfighting!" Jake cheered, jumping out of his seat. "On guard!" he shouted, whooshing a ruler through the air in front of Princess Petunia's face. "Take that! And that! And...*oof!*"

Jake yelped as Petunia elbowed him irritably, knocking the ruler out of his hand and sending it flying into the Prune's cup of coffee.

"Jake!" the Prune scolded, jumping back as coffee sprayed all over her lacy blouse. "Be careful!"

"It was her, not me!" Jake replied, outraged.

Petunia tossed her golden mane and smirked. "Better sharpen up your reflexes if you're planning to beat *me* at swordfighting," she said darkly as she stalked out of the room.

Jake hurried after her. "Oh yeah? You wait," he said. "I'm going to be brilliant with a sword. I just know it!"

CHAPTER TWO

Jake, Ned and Petunia made their way
towards the West Wing of the royal castle.
The Sports Hall, gymnasium, Olympic-sized
pool and changing rooms were all here,
with several tennis courts and playing
fields outside.

As they entered the Great Hall, they
stopped and stared. A crowd of servants, all
carrying large boxes and packages, were being
given orders by a little man in a gold suit.

"This way, please!" he shouted to two of the butlers who were carrying a heavy-looking box. "Careful with that – it's worth a million, you know! Very precious indeed! This way, just follow the signs!"

The man turned round then, and the children recognised him as Sir Archie, an art collector, and a friend of their parents. "Hello there!" he cried, waving. "Just getting ready for tomorrow's exhibition. Your parents are borrowing some of my

collection for the little show they're putting on. Should be jolly good!"

"Show?" Jake echoed blankly.

King Nicholas and Queen Caroline bustled in at that moment. "Ahh, there you are," the Queen said. "Yes, I've been meaning to tell you – we're putting on an art exhibition in the royal gallery. There will be lots of very valuable paintings in there, so from now on, that part of the castle is out of bounds to you, all right?"

"What about the throne room?" Jake asked. The throne room was just next to the gallery, and he was hoping to do some roller skating there later. The smooth waxed floor made it the perfect place to practise.

"The throne room is out of bounds too," the King replied. He lowered his great bushy eyebrows sternly, fixing Jake with his dark eyes. "Understood?"

"Understood," Jake muttered, crossing his fingers behind his back. "Anyway, we've got to hurry. Swordfighting, remember?"

Once in their tracksuits and trainers, Jake, Ned and Petunia went into the Sports Hall, where a man with broad shoulders, thick black hair and keen blue eyes was waiting for them. "Good afternoon!" he said. "My name is Alexander Pearce, international swordfighting champion."

Jake sighed happily. How he'd love to say those words about himself one day! *The name's Jake, Prince Jake, international swordfighting legend…*

"… And I'm here to teach you how to use one of these," Mr Pearce said. He held up what looked like a long, thin, metal stick, and boinked the end of it.

Jake wrinkled his nose. "What's that?"

he asked suspiciously. He gazed around the hall. There were the gym bars as usual, the goal posts, and the crate where all the basketballs were kept. But something was missing, in Jake's opinion. "And where are all the swords?"

Mr Pearce laughed. "Very good, Your Highness," he said in a jolly sort of way. "Very funny. So... Does anyone know what this is called?"

Princess Petunia stuck up her hand. She had gone very pink in the cheeks, Jake noticed, and was smiling prettily at the new teacher. "Hello," she said breathlessly. "Just wanted to introduce myself. I'm Princess Petunia, but you don't need to bother about all that Your Highness stuff. You can call me Petunia. Or Pet, for short. Or…"

"Or Lovestruck," Ned giggled behind his hand to Jake. Petunia was always getting stupid crushes.

"And I've just had my nails manicured, so I hope they won't be ruined by this swordfighting..." Petunia twittered, batting her eyelashes.

Jake was still staring at the long springy stick thing in his new teacher's hand. "No, really, Mr Pearce," he said, interrupting his sister. "Where *are* the swords?"

The smile faded from Mr Pearce's face. "You're not joking, are you?" he asked after a moment.

"No," Jake said.

"You actually thought we were going to be fighting with real swords?"

"Well…yes," Jake admitted. He had a horrible sinking feeling inside. A horrible *disappointed* feeling. This wasn't how he'd imagined the lesson going at all!

"Ahh," said Mr Pearce. "Well, I'm sorry, Your Highness, but for modern swordfighting – or *fencing,* as we tend to call it – we use these." He boinked the springy stick thing again. It was beginning to annoy Jake. "This is called a foil."

There was an awkward silence. "So… You mean…we're not going to be doing *anything* with swords?" Jake asked, his shoulders slumping. He couldn't quite believe what he was hearing.

Mr Pearce shook his head. "Afraid not," he replied. "It would be far too dangerous. We don't want any heads being chopped off, do we?"

Jake was so gutted, he couldn't speak. Deep down, he'd had a feeling that he wouldn't be allowed to actually *fight* his sister or brother with a real sword, but even so, he'd still been looking forward to having a go with one. Talk about being *foiled*! "S'pose not," he muttered through gritted teeth, looking down at his feet.

"Right-o," said Mr Pearce. "Well, if you're all ready, I shall teach you the noble art of fencing. Attack, parry, counterattack, feint!"

Petunia giggled. "I'm feeling a bit faint already," she said, blushing.

After the fencing lesson, Prince Jake left the Sports Hall with a heavy heart. It was bad enough that they were using silly, bendy, babyish foils instead of swords. But it was even *worse* that his sister had been better at fencing than he had been...and had teased him non-stop about it.

"Ooh – got you, Jake," she'd cried, jabbing at his chest with the foil, during their first practice duel. "Right in the heart. Probably would have *killed* you if it had been a real sword."

Jake had swung at her with his foil, but she'd dodged nimbly out of the way, and it had slashed uselessly through the empty air. "Can't catch me!" she'd squealed.

21

"Oh, got you again! Right in the belly this time! Your guts would be hanging out all over the place by now, don't you reckon?"

Stupid fencing. Stupid Petunia. Stupid foils, Jake thought crossly, making his way back across the castle. What a let-down. Now, more than ever, he was desperate to get his hands on a real sword!

CHAPTER THREE

Whizzzzzzz! Jake flew across the floor
a few hours later, wheels spinning on his
roller skates. This was more like it – just
the thing to cheer himself up! And yeah,
so he was roller skating in the throne
room, but he was sure his mum and dad
wouldn't find out. They were too busy
drinking champagne with Sir Archie in
the banqueting hall, right over the other
side of the castle. Besides, it wasn't as if he

was going to muck about with the boring old paintings, anyway. As if he'd waste time in the gallery, when he could be here, speeding around the room!

Whizzzzz!

How Jake loved roller skating! Skimming over the polished wooden floor, swinging around his parents' thrones, practising his speed turns at each end of the room...

Whizzzzz! Oops! Jake was so busy daydreaming he almost slammed straight into the stone wall behind the thrones. He clung to the edge of his dad's throne just in time to stop himself splatting against the wall, and whirled around the back of the throne with a bump. And then a few strange things happened, all in the blink of an eye.

Something moved beneath his fingers. The edge of the throne seemed to give way, as if his fingers were sinking straight

into the solid gold. And then there came
a loud, grating sound from underneath
the throne, and the whole thing started
to move under Jake's fingers!

"What are *you* doing in here?"

Jake almost jumped out of his skin at the voice. Oh, no! There was Princess Petunia, at the far end of the room, her arms folded across her chest and a horribly smug look on her face.

"Nothing," he muttered, pushing desperately against the throne, trying to get it back in place before she could see what he'd done. There was another grating, rumbling noise and the throne moved back with a click. Thank goodness!

Petunia began to march over. "What have you done to Dad's throne? What was that noise? Have you *broken* it?"

"No!" Jake said quickly, although secretly he wasn't so sure. He looked it over hastily, before she could get there and see for herself. It was a solid gold throne, with two twisty turrets at the top, and an elaborate design on the back and sides. *Had* he

broken it? It looked all right now, but
something had definitely happened when
he'd swung round on it. And that noise!
What had that been about?

Petunia was at Jake's side now, peering
suspiciously at the throne.

"See?" Jake blustered, his heart
thumping. "It's fine."

Petunia looked at him, eyes narrowed,
as if she didn't trust him for a second.
"What are you *doing* in here, anyway?"
she asked. "You know it's out of bounds.

If Mum and Dad knew you were in here, you'd be in big trouble. *Huge* trouble!"

Jake stuck his tongue out at her. "What about you? You're in here, too," he said. "So if you think you're going to stitch me up by telling Mum and Dad, I'll just tell on you straight back."

Petunia gave him a horrible fake smile. "Well, actually, they know that *I'm* here. Mum asked me to bring her the guest list for the show. She'd left it in the gallery by mistake." She folded her arms across her chest in a smug way. "Won't she and Dad be surprised when I go back and say that I found *you* in here?"

Jake opened and shut his mouth a few times. Sometimes he really, really hated his sister! He gritted his teeth. "Almost as surprised as Mr Pearce will be, when I tell him you *lurve* him," he managed to say in return. He scrunched up his lips.

"Kissy-kissy-kissy…"

The smile slipped from Petunia's face. "You wouldn't!" she cried in horror. "If you *dare* tell him that, I'll…!"

Now it was Jake's turn to smile. "How about this?" he said. "I won't tell Mr Pearce, if you don't tell Mum and Dad."

Petunia sighed, and tossed her hair so violently it flicked in Jake's eyes, and the overpowering smell of hairspray made his nostrils tingle. "All *right*," she muttered, stomping off.

Jake let his breath out in a sigh of relief as she left the room. Phew. He'd got away with that one – just! He gave the throne a last pat, to make sure everything was back in place, then whizzed out of the room on his roller skates. He hoped he *hadn't* broken the King's throne. He'd be in the biggest trouble of his life if he had...

CHAPTER FOUR

"Now, then," Queen Caroline began the next morning. The whole of the royal family were sitting around the breakfast table, and something about her tone of voice made Prince Jake's heart sink. Whenever the Queen spoke in that brisk way, she was *definitely* in a bossing around kind of mood.

"The exhibition starts at five o'clock this evening," the Queen began, consulting a leather clipboard next to her toast plate. "The whole castle needs to be spotless, Mrs Pinny," she said to the royal housekeeper. "The paintings should be dusted, the drapes in the reception room cleaned, and the chandeliers polished. And could you arrange for a buffet to be set out for the guests too, please?"

"With lots of cake," King Nicholas put in, licking his lips.

Mrs Pinny bobbed a little curtsey. "Me and the team are onto it already, Your Majesties," she said. "Consider everything done!"

The Queen gave her a smile. "Thank you, Mrs Pinny," she said. "And Boris, you'll be on the door tonight, receiving our guests. Please arrange for a couple of the junior butlers to take people's coats to the cloakroom, and another five or so to park people's cars. Oh, and do make sure there's enough room on the helipad for guests who are flying in."

Boris bowed so low, Jake could almost see his own reflection in the butler's shiny pink bald head. "Very good, Your Majesty," Boris said.

"And kids," the Queen said, turning her eyes to Jake, Ned and Petunia. "You are all to be polite and quiet this evening. Polite and quiet, understand? Seen but not heard, like good little royal children."

Jake groaned.

Ned put his head in his hands.

Petunia smirked. "Of course, Mum!" she said sweetly.

"And you'll have to wear something smart, too," the Queen went on. "Boys, I want you in your best suits."

"Oh, Mu-u-um," Jake moaned, but the Queen ignored him.

"Petunia, an evening dress, please," she went on.

"Of course," Petunia said, admiring her reflection in one of the solid silver spoons and pouting at herself. "Mum, is Mr Pearce invited?"

"Yes, I think so," the Queen replied. Then she turned to the King. "Oh, and Nicholas, I've booked Alfonso to cut your hair this morning. You as well, boys. You've all been looking a bit shaggy around the ears lately."

Jake groaned for a third time. Not mad Alfonso! Last time the royal barber had been in, he'd practically scalped Jake and Ned. They'd be lucky if they escaped with their ears still intact this time.

King Nicholas didn't look happy either. "What's wrong with being shaggy around the ears anyway?" he protested.

The Queen eyed him over her clipboard. "Shaggy is fine for dogs, but not for royalty!" she declared. Then she glanced at her watch. "Run along, children, chop chop! And don't forget – polite and quiet. Tonight is all about best clothes and best manners, all right?"

Jake scowled. Best clothes? Best manners?
A haircut by Mad Alfonso? This day was
getting worse by the second!

"Good morning, everyone," the Prune
said, as Jake, Ned and Petunia sat down
at their desks. "It's Royal Studies first
today, and we're going to be looking
at some of the more old-fashioned
royal traditions."

"Ms Prudence, can you teach us about
swordfighting?" Jake asked at once.
"I mean, were any of our ancestors
especially brilliant swordsmen?"

"Or swords*women*," Petunia put in.

The Prune looked pleased that Jake
seemed so interested. Usually he spent
Royal Studies lessons scribbling messages
to Prince Ned, or doodling rude pictures
on his desk. "Certainly," she replied.
"The Moranian royal family have always

been keen fighters. Hundreds of years ago, this castle was very well defended with skilled archers and swordsmen. Indeed, King Samuel the Great, an ancestor of yours who reigned in the seventeenth century, was famous worldwide for his brilliance with a sword."

"Cool," Jake said, feeling excited at the thought. "Did he have loads and loads of fights?"

"He did," the Prune replied. "The story goes that he cut both arms off the King of Vulcrania in the Battle of Bayley. Oh, and he chopped the Queen of Coltavia's head off, when she beat him in a chess match."

"He sounds awful!" said Princess Petunia, looking sickened.

"He sounds BRILLIANT!" said Jake in the same breath. "Wow. What else did he do?"

"Oh, all sorts of vile things," the Prune said. "Usually with Deathblade, of course."

"Deathblade?" put in Ned. "Who was that?"

The Prune stared at Ned in surprise. "You know, *Deathblade!*" she said. There was silence as Jake, Petunia and Ned all looked blankly at her. "My dear children," the Prune said in a hushed voice, "do you mean no one's ever told you about Deathblade, King Samuel's favourite sword?"

"No!" Jake said. "What happened? Will *you* tell us?"

"Of course," the Prune said. She cleared her throat and sat on the edge of her desk. "I can't believe you don't know this already, but anyway... King Samuel had many swords, but his favourite was a broadsword that became nicknamed 'Deathblade'.

Everyone was scared of Deathblade. King Samuel chopped off many, many heads and limbs with it. It was his most treasured possession. He used to clang it against his shield whenever he was marching into battle, and the enemy side would be scared stiff at the very sound. Until one day, that is, when the King went too far and chopped off the King of Sultana's big toe, for a dare."

"Yuck!" Jake cried in delight. "That's toe-tally disgusting!"

"He did it for a *dare*?" squeaked Petunia in shock. "What kind of a king was he, to accept a dare like that?"

"A very reckless king," the Prune replied disapprovingly. "And the King of Sultana was – quite understandably – furious! As soon as his foot had stopped bleeding, he ordered his army to seek revenge on King Samuel. He gave them a mission to steal Deathblade from the Moranian castle and have it destroyed – he knew that would hurt Samuel more than anything else."

"What happened next?" Jake urged.

"Well, word got round to Samuel of what the King of Sultana was plotting," the Prune went on. "So Samuel hid Deathblade somewhere in the castle."

"In *this* castle?" Ned asked eagerly.

The Prune nodded. "Yes," she said. "Right here, in this castle. But it has never been found. Before the Sultanans could get here, Samuel died from a mysterious illness. Some say the Queen of Sultana had arranged for his food to be poisoned, but no one is quite sure."

"So where's the sword now?" Jake asked. "Where's Deathblade?"

The Prune gave a rare smile. "That's the big question, Your Highness," she said. "Nobody knows. It was said, long ago, that King Samuel hid it in the throne room. Some even said that he had a secret hiding place specially made for it, a place which was almost impossible for anyone to find. But we may never know the truth."

Jake's mouth fell open at her words. Deathblade, in the *throne room*? A secret hiding place? Hadn't he, Jake, seen for himself that there was something strange about the King's throne when he'd been in there yesterday?

He thought hard, his skin prickling with excitement. Maybe that rumbling sound, that grating he'd heard, had been some kind of mechanism he'd triggered. Maybe he, Prince Jake, had stumbled upon Deathblade's secret hiding place!

CHAPTER FIVE

Jake was itching to go and have a look at his dad's throne again, but first he had to suffer Alfonso cutting his hair in the royal beauty salon. Alfonso wasn't a bad person, but he didn't half like a chat. On and on and on he droned – about the weather, his mum, his pet poodle, Allegra, and his favourite popstars. Then he started talking about the art exhibition.

"I can't wait to see the paintings,"
he gushed, waving his arms in the
air, and almost stabbing Jake with
the scissors he was holding. "That
Sir Archie's got some right valuable
ones, you know. Everyone's talking
about the one that cost a million –
Moaning Lisa, it's called. The paint
must be liquid gold for it to cost that
much. Can't wait to see what all the
fuss is about."

"Mmmm," said Jake, wondering
how much longer he'd have to sit
there, his head being pulled this way
and that, with those scissors flashing
dangerously near his face. He was
dying to go and check out the throne,
to see if he could find the hidden
sword. He couldn't think about
anything else right now, let alone
boring paintings.

"There," said Alfonso, brushing away the strands of hair from Jake's neck. "Looking stunning there, if I may say so, Your Highness, simply dashing!"

"Thanks," Jake said, getting to his feet. He heard heavy footsteps outside the room, then his mum and dad's voices. He leaned closer to Alfonso. "My dad really wants his nose hair plucking by the way, after you've cut his hair. Just...don't mention it before you begin. He's a bit shy about it, you see."

Alfonso nodded. "Discretion is my middle name," he said solemnly, tapping the side of his nose. "I will not utter a word."

"Oh, and if my sister has her hair done too," Jake added, unable to resist this golden opportunity, "she's quite keen on having a short back and sides, so..."

"Hello, Jake," came his mum's voice just then, as she and King Nicholas walked into the salon. "Ahh – that's better. Has Ned had his hair cut, too, Alfonso?"

Alfonso dropped into a flamboyant bow, twirling his arm in front of him with a great flourish. "Your Majesty, you're looking as ravishing as ever," he said to the Queen, once he was upright again. "And yes, I've cut His Royal Highness Prince Ned's hair already."

"Good," the Queen said, steering the King into the seat where Jake had been sitting. "Just one shaggy dog left to shear, then."

Jake bounded to the door. At last! Now was his chance to get away and check out the throne!

"Jake," his mum said quickly, before he could escape, "your suit's laid out on your bed for you. Boris is waiting to help you into it. Off you go, dear – chop chop!"

"Right," said Jake, through gritted teeth. Foiled again! When was he ever going to get his chance to sneak away to the throne room?

"So I swung round like *this*, and I put my hand *here*..." An hour or so later, Prince Jake, dressed in his smartest, most uncomfortable suit, plus a pair of roller skates, was gripping the throne to show Prince Ned what he'd done the night before, to make it move...but this time, nothing happened.

Ned looked doubtfully up at Jake. "Are you sure it moved? It wasn't some kind of...dream, was it?" he asked.

"It *definitely* moved," Jake said. He clumped backwards, then roller skated towards the throne again. "I was whizzing along like this, and must have grabbed it around here, and then there was this weird noise that came from underneath the throne – and the whole thing shifted. I swear!"

He broke off as he heard footsteps coming into the room. Then he groaned. Oh, no. Not again!

"Short, back and sides, eh?" Petunia snarled, marching over towards them, her pink spangly evening dress swishing along the floor. Her dress was so bright, Jake wished he was wearing sunglasses. "Are you having a laugh?"

Jake bit his lip. Uh-oh. His sister was practically scarlet in the face with rage – she clashed horribly with her dress! "I don't know what you're talking about," he began to say, but she gave a hollow laugh and put her hands on her hips.

"Don't give me that!" she snorted. "Alfonso told me what you'd said. 'Petunia wants a short back and sides!' As if!" she glared, jabbing a finger at him. "It's lucky I managed to get away with just a trim, he was all set to hack the whole lot off before I jumped out of the chair in time."

"It looks a bit wonky if you ask me," Ned piped up, tipping his head on one side thoughtfully.

Petunia scowled at him. "And Dad was shouting like a wounded buffalo when I went in there," she went on. "His nose was bright red, and he was clutching it as if..."

Her voice trailed away as a thought seemed to strike her. "Hang on a minute," she said, staring at the throne. "You're looking for Deathblade, aren't you? Is *that* what you're up to in here?"

Jake hesitated. The last thing he wanted was his big sister poking her beak in! "What was wrong with Dad, then?" he asked innocently, trying to change the subject back again. "Why was he shouting?"

Petunia didn't reply. She stepped nearer the throne, an excited look in her eyes. "The other night, when I found you in here, you'd done something to the throne, hadn't you?" she asked eagerly. "Have you discovered the secret hiding place?"

"No," Jake replied cagily, hoping to get rid of her. There was no way he wanted *Petunia* to find Deathblade. He couldn't let that happen!

"You said to me you thought you *had*!"
Ned said, looking confused. "I thought..."

Jake groaned. "Oh, all right, all right,"
he said grudgingly. His little brother could
never keep his mouth shut! "Yes, the
throne *did* move, all right? And yes,
I think it might have something to do
with Deathblade. But we can't get it to
move again, so..."

Petunia came over and started leaning
against the throne, pushing at it with her
shoulder. Nothing happened.

"Budge over," Jake said impatiently, barging past her. "It was something at the top here, it gave way under my fingers when I gripped it."

The three of them jostled to examine the turret of the throne that Jake had grabbed. The gold was engraved with tiny designs, all mixed in a pattern – crowns, bugles, the Moranian flag, hunting dogs, knights' helmets and...

Jake's eyes widened. "Hey!" he said, stabbing a finger at the pattern. "Look – a sword. Right there, a tiny sword."

They all peered at it. The sword was about the size of Jake's little finger and raised, rather than being engraved like the rest of the pattern. Jake's pulse quickened. "I wonder..." he said breathlessly, and pressed the sword, hoping it would be some kind of secret button.

Nothing happened. Jake's shoulders slumped. Just for a second, he'd been really sure it was the key to opening a secret compartment!

"Hold on," said Petunia. "I can't see any other swords, can you? Look, there are loads of crowns and dogs and everything – but only one sword." Her face was alight with excitement. "It's got to do *something*. Try pushing it, Jake. Or sliding it along. Or turning it round."

PRINCE JAKE 👑

Jake tried turning the tiny raised sword shape – and to his amazement, it seemed to twist round under his fingers...and then a clicking sound came from within the throne.

"Oh my goodness," Petunia said faintly.

"It's a secret catch!" Ned gasped.

Jake was so excited, he could barely think straight. His fingers trembling, he gripped the side of the throne and pulled on it, hard, like he'd done when he'd grabbed it before.

A tremendous rumbling sound started up, then a grating noise of stone sliding across stone.

Jake thought his eyes might pop out of his head as the throne began to move on the stone floor. It swung right around, so that it now pointed sideways at the Queen's throne, rather than forwards into the room...and as it did so, Jake, Petunia

58

and Ned all gasped in shock.

"There's a hatch!" Petunia said hoarsely,
pointing down at the floor.

"A trapdoor!" breathed Jake, getting to
his knees at once to examine it.

Where the throne had been standing,
they could now see a plain wooden hatch
on the floor, with a curved iron handle.

His heart pounding, Jake pulled the handle – and the hatch lifted up with a creak. They peered in, breathless with excitement, to see a flight of stone steps leading under the ground.

"A secret stairway!" Petunia gasped. "Where do you think it goes?"

Jake bent down and took off his roller skates, then dangled his legs over the hatch and dropped down onto the first step. He grinned up at his brother and sister. "Well?" he said. "Aren't you coming to find out?"

CHAPTER SIX

"Too right," Petunia said, kicking off her high heels with a grin. "Right behind you, little bro!"

Jake picked his way down the stone steps, feeling as if he were about to burst with excitement. The air was cool and musty the further down he went, as if nobody had breathed it or walked through it for hundreds of years. The thought gave Jake goosebumps.

There was just enough light shining from the hatch above for Jake to grope his way through the tunnel, but luckily Ned was wearing one of his superhero costumes *under* his suit – and it came with a pocket torch. "You go first, though," Ned said, passing the torch over with a shiver.

Jake didn't need telling twice. He flicked

on the torch, and shone it around
excitedly. The walls were rough brick and
damp to the touch, and the stone floor felt
cold and wet under his socked feet. The
torchlight made spooky shadows, and he
flinched as he put his hand straight
through a thick spider's web. Then, just
a few metres along, the tunnel ended and
Jake found himself in some kind of room.
A room full of…

"Whoa," he breathed, staring as he
shone his torch around. "Look at this lot!"

"A secret armoury!" Petunia gasped.
"Oh my goodness!"

"Swords!" Ned said gleefully. "Shields!
Wow!"

"And…" Jake's mouth went dry as his
eyes fell upon the most enormous
broadsword he had ever seen. "Whoa," he
said again, reaching through the gloom to
pick it up. "This has got to be Deathblade!"

He was almost too excited to hold it. It weighed an absolute *ton* and lay across his arms like a huge silver beast. "Wow," he kept saying, staring at its solid blade and jewelled hilt. "Now *that's* a sword." He gazed at it in delight, and shone the torch all over it, not quite able to believe he was actually holding it. Was that really a trace of dried *enemy blood* that

Jake could see at its tip? Cool! "I can't *believe* we've—" he began, but Petunia held up a warning hand.

"Sssshhhh!" she hissed. "What's that?"

They fell silent and listened.

"So I'll cause a distraction, then you run and grab it," they heard a faint voice say. A male voice.

"Where's that coming from?" Jake whispered, staring around. He played the torchlight around the room and suddenly saw what looked like a doorway across the other side of the armoury room. He picked his way through the shields and armour pieces towards it. Yes! He was right!

The doorway opened to a narrow flight of stone steps, leading up. Jake climbed them quickly, his heart thudding as the voices grew louder. Two voices, both male.

"You know where the *Moaning Lisa* is, don't you?" one said.

"Course I do! Right slap bang in the middle of the room, idiot!" the other snapped.

Jake frowned to himself as he reached the top of the steps. There was a small stone landing there, but nowhere further to go. He was surrounded by crumbling brick walls, with just a chink of light shining through one of them, high up. He peered through it – and gasped as he saw two pairs of feet in front of him. The chink of light was actually a secret spyhole that looked into the corridor just outside the gallery room!

He beckoned Ned and Petunia up, putting his finger on his lips to warn them to be quiet. Then he showed them the gap and they all listened through it.

"Well, watch out for the butlers," the first voice said in a warning tone. "They've been guarding it all day. But when I set the fire alarms off, that'll get them out of the gallery pretty quick."

"Then I'll rush in, nab *Moaning Lisa*, get it down the back staircase and into the van," gloated the second voice. "Job done!"

Jake gazed at his brother and sister in shock. These men were plotting to steal the *Moaning Lisa*! The painting that Alfonso had said was worth a million!

Petunia put her hands on her hips. "What a cheek!" she hissed.

Jake nodded. "We've got to stop them," he whispered, stepping away from the spy hole so they wouldn't be heard.

"How, though?" Petunia whispered back.

Nobody could think of anything. The three of them crept down to the armoury room again, still thinking hard. And then Jake had a brilliant idea. "With Deathblade, of course!" he said.

Ned's eyes boggled. "You're going to chop their heads off?" he asked, sounding eager.

Jake picked up the heavy broadsword and slowly raised it above his head with a grin. "No," he admitted, slightly reluctantly. "But we can give them a good

scare with it, I reckon, don't you?"

Petunia picked a helmet and wiped the cobwebs off it with a look of disgust before putting it on her head. Then she giggled. "Remember what Ms Prudence said about King Samuel banging Deathblade against his shield as he marched into battle? How it scared everyone by making such a noise?" Her eyes shone in the torchlight as she held up a sword and shield. "Attack, parry, counterattack, feint!" she chanted, swishing her sword through the air. "Let's do it!"

Jake rammed a helmet on his own head, then grabbed a huge tarnished shield for himself, while Ned gathered together a rusty chestplate, sword and shield. Sometimes, thought Jake, his sister was actually pretty cool. "Too right," he said. "Come on!"

CHAPTER SEVEN

Jake, Ned and Petunia hurried back along the secret tunnel and clambered out through the trapdoor into the throne room. "Let's do it," said Jake.

CRASH! BANG! SMASH!

CLANG! CLANG! CLANG!

The three of them strode forwards, towards the gallery.

WHACK! WALLOP! CLASH!

CLANG! CLANG! CLANG!

Jake was having a great time whacking Deathblade against his shield as hard as he possibly could. It made the most amazing racket he'd ever heard. Either side of him, Petunia and Ned were doing the same. What would the Queen say if she could see how polite and quiet her children were being now? Jake grinned at the thought. Seen but not heard? Not exactly…

CRASH! BANG! SMASH!

CLANG! CLANG! CLANG!

If Jake closed his eyes, he could almost imagine he *was* King Samuel the Great, striding out to war with his trusty broadsword, ready to do some serious head-chopping…

"There they are!" bellowed Petunia over the din. "There!"

Jake jolted out of his thoughts to see two men outside the gallery, looking terrified at the sight of him, Petunia and Ned. Then he remembered the brilliant daydream he'd had just the day before...

He clasped the hilt of the silver sword, his eyes locked on the men's scared faces. "Trying to steal the *Moaning Lisa*, were you?" he hissed, taking a step forward. "You've done it now. You should never have come here." He raised the sword and pointed it menacingly. "Now it's time to *pay*!"

"Wait!" one of the men yelped. "Please – I beg you! Show some mercy!"

"No chance, loser," snarled Jake. He swung the sword through the air, the heavy silver blade swishing, and...

"What is going on? Jake! Put that down at once!"

Rats! His mum, dad and Sir Archie? What were *they* doing here?

"You should ask these two what's going on," Petunia said, pushing her helmet off and shaking out her hair. "They were just about to pinch the *Moaning Lisa!*"

"And *we* stopped them!" Jake boasted.

"*What?*" Sir Archie bellowed. "Trying to steal the *Moaning Lisa*?"

"Run for it!" one of the men shouted, looking terrified, and they both pelted down the corridor.

"Come back!" yelled Jake, with another fearful clang of Deathblade against his shield as he chased after them.

But further down the corridor, Boris had appeared in front of the burglars, with Bert, another of the butlers, blocking their way. At the same time, Jake and the rest of the family had charged behind them, which meant the men were trapped.

"I think you'd better come with us," Boris said grimly as he and Bert hauled the burglars away.

By now, quite a crowd had gathered, drawn by the commotion. There were servants as well as the guests for the art show, all staring at the royal children. Jake suddenly realised just how dusty his smart trousers were, and that his jacket had a new jaggedy rip at one elbow. Petunia and Ned were almost as bad, their faces covered in streaks of dirt. Jake had never seen his sister in quite such a state.

Jake held his breath. They might have just saved the *Moaning Lisa* from being stolen, but they had ruined their best clothes and been anything but polite and quiet. *Uh-oh. Here comes a right royal telling-off,* he thought glumly.

Suddenly a figure bustled through the crowd. The Prune in her best flowery dress, her eyes gleaming delightedly through her spectacles. "It's not... You didn't... Did you really find...?" she said, not able to finish her questions in her excitement.

Jake grinned and raised Deathblade in the air. "It is," he said solemnly. "We found it, Deathblade! Isn't it wicked?"

"There's a whole secret armoury room!" Petunia added.

"And a secret tunnel, too!" Ned burst out.

And then everyone was gasping and smiling, and coming over to see Deathblade and the other armour for themselves.

"My goodness, what a beast!" King Nicholas whistled, slapping Jake on the back joyfully. "Nice work, Jake. And seeing off those burglars, as well! King Samuel would have been very proud."

The Queen beamed at them. "Such brave children!" she exclaimed. "We'll have Deathblade put up as part of the exhibition. I know everyone will want to see it. Well done!"

"Quite extraordinary," Sir Archie added. "And saving my *Moaning Lisa*, too. Bravo, children. Bravo, Your Highnesses!"

Even Mr Pearce was there, his face

lighting up at the sight of such a tremendous sword. "Wow," he said reverently. "You know, Jake," he went on, "once you're really good at using the foil, we could see about you having some lessons using Deathblade. I'm sure King Samuel would have wanted that."

Jake felt his grin stretch from ear to ear. "Oh, thanks, Mr Pearce!" he cried. "That would be brilliant!"

King Nicholas winked at his children as the Queen started ushering her guests into the gallery. "Can't wait to get this exhibition over with, so that I can explore that armoury room," he said in a low voice. "This is such a find, kids. Such a find for our royal family!"

"And such a relief that my painting is safe," Sir Archie added. "Once you've cleaned yourself up, you must come and look at it for yourself, and have some cakes.

79

There's a fantastic buffet in there,
you know."

"Are there any *sword*fish sandwiches?"
Ned giggled.

Jake was still grinning, feeling as if he
might very well explode with joy. Swords,
secret tunnels, foiling burglars and now
cakes. Did life get any better than that?
He twirled Deathblade around happily.
"Thanks, Sir Archie, that sounds brilliant,"
he said, then turned to Ned and Petunia.
"Come on, you two. *Chop chop!*"

The *Prince Jake* books are available from all good bookshops,
or can be ordered direct from the publisher:
Orchard Books, PO BOX 29, Douglas IM99 1BQ.
Credit card orders please telephone 01624 836000 or fax 01624 837033 or visit our
website: www.orchardbooks.co.uk or e-mail: bookshop@enterprise.net for details.
To order please quote title, author and ISBN and your full name and address.
Cheques and postal orders should be made payable to 'Bookpost plc.'
Postage and packing is FREE within the UK
(overseas customers should add £2.00 per book).
Prices and availability are subject to change.